BOYZ RULE!

Water Rats

Felice Arena and Phil Kettle

illustrated by
Susy Boyer

MACMILLAN

First published 2003 by
MACMILLAN EDUCATION AUSTRALIA PTY LTD
627 Chapel Street, South Yarra 3141

Associated companies and representatives throughout the world.

National Library of Australia
Cataloguing-in-Publication data

Arena, Felice.
  Water rats.

  For primary school children.
  ISBN 0 7329 8956 6.

  1. Swimming pools – Juvenile literature. I. Kettle,
  Phil. II. Title. (Series: Arena, Felice. Boyz rule).

A823.3

Project management by Limelight Press Pty Ltd
Cover and text design by Lore Foye
Illustrations by Susy Boyer

Printed in Australia by McPherson's Printing Group

ISBN 0 7329 8956 6
ISBN 0 7329 9178 1 (Set)

Contents

Tom   Joey

CHAPTER 1

Warm-up Race

Joey and Tom are standing at the
edge of their local public swimming
pool. While their mothers are chatting
under the shade of a nearby tree,
Joey and Tom look at each other, grin,
nod and then suddenly leap into
the pool.

Joey "Awwwh! It's freezing!"

Tom "Yeah, how can it be so cold?
It's 100 degrees today!"

Joey "I know. Look! I've got a million
goose bumps on my arms. Let's try
to get a bit warmer. I'll race you to
the steps over there."

Tom "Okay."

Joey "Ready, set, go!"

Joey and Tom thrash their arms about, swimming as fast as they can. They both reach the steps at the same time.

Joey "I'm the winner! I'm world champion! I'm Ian Thorpe!"

Tom "No you're not. It was a draw. And if you're Ian Thorpe, who am I then?"

Joey "You're Grant Hackett—
because he always comes second
to Thorpey."

Tom "But I *didn't* come second. It
was a *draw*."

Joey "And I've got big feet like
Ian Thorpe. My feet are much
bigger than yours!"

Tom "Yeah, and so's your head!
Let's race again."

Joey "Nah."

Tom "Why? You scared I'll beat you this time?"

Joey "No."

Tom "Why then?"

Joey "Because I'm not cold anymore. My goose bumps are gone."

CHAPTER 2

Tom, Joey and Marco

Joey and Tom decide to play a game instead.

Tom "What will we play?"

Joey "Marco Polo."

Tom "Okay. So how do you play that again?"

Joey "Well if I'm 'it', I have to close my eyes and keep them closed while I try to find you. When I call out 'Marco', you have to answer 'Polo', so I can hear where your voice is coming from.

When I find you, it's your turn to be 'it'. Okay? I'll be 'it' first. The only rule is you're not allowed to leave the shallow area, 'cause I'm not allowed in the deep end."

Tom "Got it! But just one question."

Joey "What?"

Tom "Who was Marco Polo?"

Joey "He was a famous Italian. I think he was the first person to invent pizzas!"

Tom "That's cool—I love pizza!"

Joey "Me too. Let's start."

Tom quickly swims away from Joey, while Joey wades through the water with his eyes closed.

Joey "Marco!"
Tom "Polo!"
Joey "Marco!"
Tom "Polo!"
Joey "Marco!"
Joey "Marco!"
Joey "I said '*Marco*'!!!"
Joey "Tom! *I said 'Marco'*!!! You have to say '*Polo*'!"
Joey "Tom?"

CHAPTER 3

Pee Is for Pool

Joey looks in every direction—Tom
has disappeared. Suddenly Joey sees
him running from the toilet block,
back towards the pool. Tom leaps
back into the water, landing only
centimetres away from Joey.

Tom "Polo!"

Joey "You can't say 'Polo' now! You left the game. You can't do that."

Tom "I was busting to go. I almost did it in the water. But I didn't— 'cause you know what happens if you pee in here?"

Joey "What?"

Tom "The water turns red. Then everyone knows that you've just peed. Wouldn't you just die?"

Joey "That doesn't really happen."

Tom "Yes it does."

Joey "No it doesn't."

Tom "It does! It's true."

Joey "No it isn't."

Tom "Yes it is. There's some special chemical they put in the chlorine that makes it do that."

Joey "I don't think so."

Tom "Well it's the truth."

Joey "No it isn't."

Tom "How can you be so sure?"

Joey "Because I'm peeing right now."

Tom "Ewwww! Next to me? Gross."

Joey "I'm joking!! I haven't."

CHAPTER 4

Deep Dive Discovery

Tom splashes Joey. Joey splashes
Tom. Both boys end up in an all-out
"splash battle".

Joey "Okay stop! Stop! You got me!
Let's go to the deep end."

Tom "But I thought you said you
weren't allowed in the deep end?"

Joey "I'm not. But our mums aren't looking. They're busy talking. They won't even notice we're gone."

Tom "I'm not sure. I'm not a real strong swimmer."

Joey "Yes you are—you're Ian Thorpe!"

Tom "I thought I was Grant Hackett?"

Joey "Come on! We'll creep along the edge of the pool. You won't even have to let go."

Tom "Okay. You go first."

Grabbing onto the side of the pool, Joey and Tom slowly edge their way to the deep end.

Joey "See—nothing to worry about."

Tom "I wonder how deep it is?"

Joey "Really deep. About three times as long as us. I'm going to see if I can touch the bottom."

Tom "But ... aren't you scared?"

Joey "Nup."

Joey dives under the water while Tom continues to hold on tightly to the pool's edge. Joey suddenly comes up, bursting for air.

Tom "Did you make it?"

Joey "Yeah. My ears popped. And look!"

Tom "It's a gold ring."

Joey "I found it on the bottom—I'm rich."

Joey slides the gold ring onto his
thumb—it fits perfectly.

Tom "What are you going to do with
  it?"
Joey "I'll sell it and make loads of
  money."
Tom "Shouldn't you hand it in?"
Joey "Yeah, you're probably right.
  Maybe I'll get a reward."

Tom "Like what?"

Joey "A hundred dollars—or even more."

Tom "Wow!"

Joey "I can buy some goggles. And flippers. And a black bodysuit like Ian Thorpe. And ..."

Tom "Will you buy me something?"

Joey "Um ... well, no. I'll have to give some to Mum for food and stuff."

Tom "Oh."

Joey "But you'll be able to wear one of my flippers."

Tom "Cool!"

Joey "Let's swim across to the other side."

Tom "But it's deep. And what about the ring?"

Joey "I'll hand it in later. Come on, let's go!"

Tom "Are we gonna swim across the deep part?"

Joey "Yeah, don't worry. You can do it. We'll dog paddle. Come on. We've just escaped from an island prison camp. And we have to swim to the mainland to get away from the enemy."

Joey paddles out across the pool heading towards the other side. Tom reluctantly follows.

Joey "That's it! Stick by my side. And don't worry that it's deep. We can't let the enemy get us—or the sharks."

Tom "Sharks?"

Joey "Keep paddling. We're almost there. Oh no! The enemy have just found out we've escaped. They're sending out their search planes after us. Paddle faster!"

CHAPTER 5

Poolside Drama

Out of nowhere a large boy suddenly charges for the pool and leaps towards Joey and Tom. He hits the water with a giant belly flop, creating an enormous wave, which crashes over the top of them.

Joey "Oh no! We're being bombed! The enemy has found us. Hurry Tom. We're nearly there."

Tom "I'm getting tired. I don't think I can ..."

Joey "Don't give up now! Come on! Only a few more strokes."

Tom "Joey! I can't ..."

Joey "Yahoo! We've made it!" Freedom is ours! We outsmarted the enemy and ... Tom?"

Joey has made it to the other side of the pool. Once again he turns to see Tom is nowhere to be seen.

Joey "Oh no—he's drowned."

Joey hurriedly swims back out to the middle of the deep end and dives below just as Tom pops up behind him. When Joey comes up for air he discovers that Tom is sitting on the other side of the pool, propped up on the edge, smirking to himself. Joey swims over to him.

Joey "That's not funny. I thought you sank or something."

Tom "I decided to swim to the mainland underwater—so the enemy wouldn't see me."

Joey "I thought you were scared of the deep?"

Tom "Tricked ya!"

Joey "I can't believe you did that. That's a bad joke."

Tom "Sorry."

Joey "Oh no! I don't believe it."

Tom "I said I'm sorry."

Joey "No, not that. My ring—it's gone."

The boys look around desperately.

Joey "We have to go back out there. And you have to help me look for the ring—now that I know you're not scared of the deep."

Tom "Do I get some of the reward then?"

Joey "No."

Tom "Then I don't want to help."

Joey "Okay, okay. You can have the flippers."

Tom "And … ?"

Joey "And you can be Ian Thorpe—always!"

Tom "Cool. Let's go and find it."

Joey and Tom swim back out to the middle of the deep end. Suddenly their mothers discover that the boys are in the deep end.

"Tom! Joey! Get out of the water—*now*!" they angrily yell from the edge of the pool.

The boys' mothers are really mad and decide to go home. Joey and Tom are now sitting quietly in the back seat of Tom's mum's car.

Joey "Sorry I made you follow me to the deep end."

Tom "I'm sorry that you lost the gold ring."

Joey "Yeah, well I'm sorry I called you Grant Hackett."

Tom "Yeah. I'm *also* sorry I called you Grant Hackett. *You* should be Ian Thorpe."

Joey "Thanks. You know what else I'm sorry about?"

Tom "What?"

Joey looks up at his mum and
Tom's mother seated at the front of
the car.

Joey "I'm sorry we got caught by
the enemy."

Tom "Me too. Do you want to
escape when we get back home ...
er, I mean prison?"

Joey "You bet!"

Tom

BOYZ RULE!
Pool Lingo

Joey

bomb A way of jumping into the pool that makes big waves. Doing bombs is banned in public pools.

freestyle The most common swimming style used in pools.

swimming carnival When a group of swimmers swim against each other in different events.

toilets Where you should go before you get into the pool.

BOYZ RULE!
Pool Must-dos

☞ Make sure you can swim before you jump into the deep end.

☞ Don't eat before you go swimming—you might sink to the bottom of the pool like a rock.

☞ Don't pee in the pool—there are toilets for that.

☞ Make sure that an adult knows you are at the swimming pool.

☞ If you have a gap between your front teeth, learn how to squirt water through it like a water pistol.

☞ Make sure that your board shorts are tied up properly before you dive in—you don't want to lose them!

☞ Don't run around the edge of the swimming pool or you might fall over, hit your head and fall into the pool.

☞ Always remember to put on plenty of sunscreen before you go swimming.

BOYZ RULE!

Pool Instant Info

The largest swimming pool in the world is in Casablanca, Morocco. It is 480 metres long and 75 metres wide.

Martin Strel, from Slovenia, swam 3004 kilometres—the greatest distance ever swum by a single swimmer—in August 2000.

The most rotations possible under water in one breath is 28.

The most swimmers to swim in a one-hour swimathon is 2533.

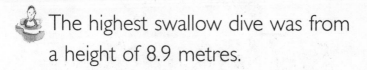 The highest swallow dive was from a height of 8.9 metres.

 Swimming has been an Olympic sport for men since 1896.

Swimming became an Olympic sport for women in 1912.

Swimming is the second largest sport in the Olympic Games.

BOYZ RULE!

Think Tank

1 What is butterfly?

2 How many laps do you have to swim in a 1500 metre race, if the pool is 50 metres in length?

3 What can make you swim faster?

4 If someone says that they swim like a rock, what do they do?

5 What is the best swimming nation in the world?

6 What colour are the medals that Ian Thorpe usually gets when he wins swimming races?

7 What is Ian Thorpe's nickname?

8 Is swimming good exercise?

Answers

1 Butterfly is a swimming stroke.

2 You have to do 30 laps.

3 If you wear flippers you'll swim faster—just think how fast dolphins can swim.

4 They sink to the bottom of the pool when they try to swim.

5 Australia, of course!!!

6 Gold, gold, gold is the colour of Ian Thorpe's medals.

7 Ian Thorpe's nickname is The Thorpedo.

8 Yes, swimming really is good exercise.

How did you score?

- If you got 8 correct answers, you might be ready for the Australian swimming team.

- If you got 6 correct answers, keep training and you could make it.

- If you got fewer than 4 answers correct, make sure that you don't get out of the wading pool.

Felice → ← Phil

Hi Guys!

We have heaps of fun reading and want you to, too. We both believe that being a good reader is really important and so cool.

Try out our suggestions to help you have fun as you read.

At school, why don't you use "Water Rats" as a play and you and your friends can be the actors. Set the scene for your play. Put some sunscreen on or hang your favourite towel over your shoulder. Or use your imagination to pretend that you are at the pool, ready to have some pool fun.

So ... have you decided who is going to be Joey and who is going to be Tom? Now, with your friends, read and act out our story in front of the class.

We have a lot of fun when we go to schools and read our stories. After we finish the kids all clap really loudly. When you've finished your play your classmates will do the same. Just remember to look out the window—there might be a talent scout from a television station watching you!

Reading at home is really important and a lot of fun as well.

Take our books home and get someone in your family to read them with you. Maybe they can take on a part in the story.

Remember, reading is a whole lot of fun.

So, as the frog in the local pond would say, Read-it!

And remember, Boyz Rule!

When We Were Kids

Felice

Phil

Phil "What was your favourite swimming stroke when you were a kid?"

Felice "Butterfly. I loved to pretend that I was a dolphin, especially because you do the dolphin kick in butterfly."

Phil "Did you ever win any major races?"

Felice "Yep, when I was thirteen I broke the state record for 50-metre butterfly."

Phil "So what was your nickname … Flipper?"

Felice "No, but I do have cravings to eat tuna every day."

What a Laugh!

Q What did the Olympic sneezing champion win?

A A cold medal.

BOYZ RULE!

Read about the fun
that boys have in these
BOYZ RULE! titles:

Park Soccer

Golf Legends

Yabby Hunt

The Tree House

Bike Daredevils

Camping Out

Gone Fishing

Water Rats

and more ... !